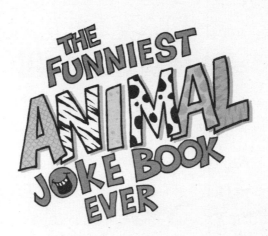

THE FUNNIEST ANIMAL JOKE BOOK EVER

Collect them all!

The Funniest Holiday Joke Book Ever

The Funniest Back to School Joke Book Ever

The Funniest Spooky Joke Book Ever

The Funniest Christmas Joke Book Ever

The Funniest Football Joke Book Ever

THE FUNNIEST ANIMAL JOKE BOOK EVER

By Joe King

Illustrated by Nigel Baines

Andersen Press

This edition first published
in Great Britain in 2015 by
ANDERSEN PRESS
20 Vauxhall Bridge Road
London SW1V 2SA
www.andersenpress.co.uk

British Library Cataloguing in
Publication Data available.

ISBN 978 1 78344 233 1

Printed and bound by
CPI Group (UK) Ltd, Croydon, CR0 4YY

On the Farm

**What did one pig say
to the other?**
'Let's be pen pals.'

1

**What do sheep do
on sunny days?**
Have a baa-baa-cue

**What is a horse's
favourite sport?**
Stable tennis

**What happened when the
cows got out of their field?**
There was udder chaos

**What happened to the chick
that misbehaved at school?**
It was eggspelled

**What do you call
a sleeping bull?**
A bull-dozer

How do you arrest a pig?
Put him in ham cuffs

**What's a cow's favourite
love song?**
*'When I Fall In Love It
Will Be For Heifer'*

**What do you get if you
cross a chicken with a cow?**
Roost beef

**What do you get if you
cross a cow with a mule?**
Milk with a kick in it

BOY: Did you know it takes
three sheep to make a jumper?
GIRL: *I didn't know
sheep could knit.*

**What musical key
do cows sing in?**
Beef flat

How do sheep keep warm?
Central bleating

What animal says 'OO'?
A cow with no lips

**What did the mummy cow
say to the baby cow?**
'It's way pasture bedtime.'

**What did the boy sheep
say to the girl sheep
on Valentine's Day?**
'Wool you be mine?'

**Where do sheep
do on holiday?**
The Baaaaahamas

Where do horses live?
In the neigh-bourhood

**How do sheep sign
their letters?**
'Ewes sincerely.'

**What do sheep say
at Christmas?**
'Season's Bleatings!'

**What's the slowest horse
in the world?**
A clothes-horse

**What do you get if you cross a
pig with a naked person?**
Streaky bacon

**What kind of animal
goes OOM?**
A cow walking backwards

**How do you fit more pigs
on your farm?**
Build a sty-scraper

What did the farmer call the cow that had no milk?
An udder failure

What do you get from a pampered cow?
Spoiled milk

Knock, knock
Who's there?
Goat
Goat who?
Goat the door and find out

What is the easiest way to count a herd of cattle?
With a cowculator

What does a pig put on his paper cut?
An oinkment

What is a cow's favourite programme?
Dr Moo

Where do cows go with their friends?
To the moo-vies

PATIENT: Doctor, Doctor, I've
just swallowed a sheep
DOCTOR: *How do you feel?*
PATIENT: Very baa-aaa-d!

**How do cows sneak
off a farm?**
Right pasteurize

PATIENT: Doctor, Doctor,
I feel like a goat.
DOCTOR: *How long have
you felt like that?*
PATIENT: Ever since I was a kid.

**What do you call a cow that
won't give milk?**
A milk dud

Knock Knock!
Who's there?
Cowsgo
Cowsgo who?
No, cows go moo!

**Where does a cow go
on holiday?**
To an aMOOsement park

**What did the horse say
when he fell?**
I've fallen and I can't giddy up

PATIENT: Doctor, Doctor,
people think I'm a cow
DOCTOR: *Pull the udder one*

**What do you call a cow
in a tornado?**
A milkshake

Why do cows wear bells?
Because their horns don't work

**What kind of tie does
a pig wear?**
A pigsty

**What has two arms, two
wings, two tails, three heads,
three bodies and eight legs?**
*A farmer on a horse
holding a chicken*

All Creatures Great and Small

What time is it when an elephant sits on your fence?
Time to get a new fence

**What do Paddington Bear
and Winnie the Pooh pack
on their holidays?**
The bear essentials

**What do you call an
exploding monkey?**
A baboom

**What do you call
a messy hippo?**
A hippopota-mess

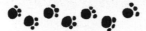

**On which day do lions
eat people?**
Chewsday

**What do camels use
to hide themselves?**
Camelflauge

**What's the difference
between a reindeer
and a snowball?**
*They're both brown,
except the snowball*

What's the difference between an injured lion and a wet day?
One pours with rain, the other roars with pain

What's black and white and makes a lot of noise?
A zebra with a set of drums

**What do you call a bear
with no teeth?**
A gummy bear

**What's black and white,
and black and white,
and black and white?**
A panda rolling down a hill

**What do you get if you cross
Bambi with a ghost?**
Bamboo

**Where did the mouse
park his boat?**
At the hickory dickory dock

How does a lion greet the other animals in the field?
'Pleased to eat you!'

What do you get if you cross a tiger with a snow man?
Frostbite

Knock, knock
Who's there?
Rhino
Rhino who?
Rhino every knock knock joke there is

How do you stop a skunk from smelling?
You hold its nose

**What do you call a deer
with no eyes?**
No idea

**What do you call a deer
with no eyes and no legs?**
Still no idea

**What has six eyes
but cannot see?**
Three blind mice

**How does a hedgehog
play leap-frog?**
Very carefully

**What do you call a
T-Rex's bruise?**
A dino-sore

**What do you call a gorilla
wearing ear-muffs?**
*Anything you like – he
can't hear you*

**What do you give an elephant
that's about to sneeze?**
Plenty of space

**What do you get when you
cross an elephant and rhino?**
'Ell-if-I-know

**How do you know if there is
an elephant under the bed?**
Your nose is touching the ceiling

What did the judge say when the skunk walked into the courtroom?
Odour in the court

Who was the gorilla's favourite American president?
Ape-reham Lincoln

**What mouse was
a Roman emperor?**
Julius Cheeser

**How do you keep an
elephant in suspense?**
I'll tell you tomorrow

**What did the peanut
say to the elephant?**
Nothing, peanuts don't talk

**Why do gorillas have
big nostrils?**
Because they have big fingers

**How can you tell if you've had
an elephant in your fridge?**
It leaves footprints in the butter

It's obvious that animals are smarter than humans. Put eight horses in a race and 20,000 people will go along to see it. But put eight people in a race and not one horse will bother to go along and watch.

What do you get if you cross a kangaroo with a sheep?
A woolly jumper

Why did the elephant cross the road?
To pick up the flattened chicken

What do you call a bear with no ear?
B

**Why do elephants
never forget?**
*Because no one ever
tells them anything*

**Why didn't the boy mouse
like the girl mouse?**
They just didn't click

Why don't bears wear socks?
*Because they like to walk
on their bear feet*

Why do skunks argue?
*Because they like to
kick up a stink*

PENGUIN: What's your name?
POLAR BEAR: *My name
is . . . Stuart.*
PENGUIN: Why the large pause?
POLAR BEAR: *I've
always had them*

**What kind of bears like to go
out in the rain?**
Drizzly bears

Did you phone the zoo today?
Yes, but I couldn't get through
because the lion's busy.

Why did the tortoise
cross the road?
To get to the shell station

How did the rabbit
propose to his girlfriend?
With a 14 carrot ring

Knock, knock
Who's there?
Panther
Panther who?
My panther falling down

**Why did the lion spit
out the clown?**
Because he tasted funny

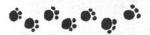

**What do you get when
you cross a porcupine
with a balloon?**
POP!

**What animals are on
legal documents?**
Seals

**How does a mouse feel
after it takes a shower?**
Squeaky clean

**Why are teddy bears
never hungry?**
They are always stuffed

What is 'out of bounds'?
An exhausted kangaroo

**What is a cheetah's
favourite food?**
Fast food

**What do you call a
dinosaur in a car crash?**
A tyrannosaurus wreck

**Why didn't the boy
believe the tiger?**
He thought it was a lion

What do you get when you cross a giraffe with an ant?
A giant

What did the banana do when the monkey chased it?
The banana split

**What's worse than a
centipede with athlete's foot?**
A porcupine with split ends

**Why are lions so
slow to apologise?**
*It takes them a long time to
swallow their pride*

**How did Noah see the
animals in the Ark at night?**
With flood lighting

**Why is it hard to play
cards in the jungle?**
There are too many cheetahs

**Why did the witches' team
lose the baseball game?**
Because their bats flew away

**What sound does a
grape make when an
elephant steps on it?**
None, it just lets out a little wine

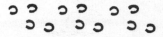

**What did the mummy
buffalo say to her son
before he went to school?**
'Bison!'

Creepy Crawlies

What insect runs away from everything?
A flee

Why do bees have sticky hair?
Because they use honeycombs

What is a snail?
A slug with a crash helmet

**What's the difference
between a coyote and a flea?**
*One howls on the prairie, and the
other prowls on the hairy*

**What did the earwig say when
he fell off the table?**
'Ere we go again

**What did the spider do
on the computer?**
It made a website

If a fly and a flea pass each other, what time is it?
Fly past flea

Why did the man throw the butter out of the window?
Because he wanted to see a butterfly

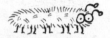

What are caterpillars afraid of?
Dogerpillars

Alex's class went on
a nature ramble.
'What do you call a thing with
ten legs, red spots and great
big jaws, sir?' asked Alex.
'I've no idea, why do you
ask?' replied the teacher.
'Because one just crawled up
your trouser leg!'

Why don't centipedes
play football?
*Because by the time they've got
their boots on, it's time to go home*

**Why couldn't the
butterfly go to the dance?**
Because it was a moth-ball

**What do you call a
fly without wings?**
A walk

Knock, knock
Who's there?
Spider
Spider who?
**You tried to hide her,
but I spider!**

**What do you get if you cross a
bumble bee with a doorbell?**
A humdinger

**What do you call
a clever insect?**
A spelling bee

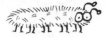

Where do bees go on holiday?
Stingapore

**What do you call a bee that is
always complaining?**
A grumble bee

**Why was the centipede
late for school?**
*Because he was playing 'This
Little Piggy' with his baby brother*

**What did the flea say
to his girlfriend?**
'I love you aw-flea!'

Why don't anteaters get sick?
Because they're full of anty-bodies

What did one worm say to the other when he was late home?
'Where on earth have you been?'

What did one flea say to the other flea?
'Shall we walk or take the dog?'

What is the strongest animal?
A snail – he carries his house on his back

What did the dog say after his bath?
'Long time no flea!'

**How do you find where
a flea has bitten you?**
Start from scratch

How do bees get to school?
By school buzz

**A guy hears a knock on his
door. He opens the door, sees
a snail, then picks it up and
chucks it as far as possible.
Three years later, he hears a
knock on his door, opens the
door, and sees the same snail.
The snail says, 'Hey, what did
you do that for?!'**

**What medicine do you
give to a sick termite?**
Ant-i-biotics

What games do ants play with elephants?
Squash

What do bugs like to sleep on?
A caterpillow

What does a caterpillar do on New Years' Day?
Turn over a new leaf

**What is green, sooty
and whistles when it rubs
its back legs together?**
Chimney Cricket

**What has antlers and
sucks blood?**
A moose-quito

**What's the difference
between school dinners
and a pile of slugs?**
School dinners come on a plate

**What did the slug say to the
snail when he ran him over?**
'I'll get you next slime!'

**What speed was the snail
doing on the motorway?**
About one mile a week

**How do snails get their
shells to shine?**
They use snail varnish

**What do you do when
two snails have a fight?**
Leave them to slug it out

**Where do you
find giant snails?**
At the ends of giants' fingers

**Who comes to a picnic
but is never invited?**
A Wasp

Why are As like flowers?
Because bees come after them

Why was the ant confused?
Because all his uncles were ants

**What's on the ground and also
a hundred feet in the air?**
A centipede on its back

**What's worse than a
worm in your apple?**
Half a worm

**What kind of fly has
a sore throat?**
A hoarse fly

**What do you call two ants
that run away to get married?**
Ant-elopes

Furry Friends

**Why did the dog
sit in the shade?**
*Because he didn't want
to be a hot dog*

**What happened when
the cat ate a lemon?**
He became a sour puss

What is a cat's favourite song?
Three Blind Mice

**What's a dog's favourite
kind of pizza?**
Pupperoni

**How do you stop a dog
barking in the back
seat of a car?**
Put him in the front seat

**What is the quietest
kind of a dog?**
A hush puppy

**Where do hamsters
come from?**
Hamsterdam

**What do you get if you
cross a cocker spaniel,
a poodle and a cockerel?**
Cockerpoodledoo

**What do you call
a happy Lassie?**
A jolly collie

**What do you get when
you pour hot water
down a rabbit hole?**
Hot cross bunnies

**How do you spell mousetrap
using just three letters?**
C-A-T

**What is a dog's
favourite food?**
Everything on your plate

**How do you know that carrots
are good for the eyes?**
*Have you ever seen a
rabbit with glasses?*

**What do you call a cat that
has just eaten a whole duck?**
A duck-filled fatty puss

**There are two cats. One called
One Two Three and the other
called Un Deux Trois. They
had a race across the English
Channel. Who won?**
*One Two Three cat because Un
Deux Trois cat cinq*

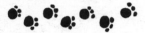

**What did the stupid man
call his pet tiger?**
Spot

**What do you get if you cross a
leopard with a watchdog?**
A terrified postman

**What kind of dog can
always tell the time?**
A watchdog

**What do you do if your dog
chews your dictionary?**
Take the words out of his mouth

**What does a cat say when
somebody steps on its tail?**
'Me-oww!'

**Why was the cat
afraid of a tree?**
Because of the bark

**A man went into his local
department store and saw a
sign on the escalator: 'Dogs
must be carried on this
escalator.' The silly man then
spent the next two hours
looking for a dog.**

**What kinds of cats
love water?**
Octopusses

**How do you make
a goldfish old?**
Take away the 'g'

**Why don't dogs
make good dancers?**
Because they have two left feet

**What do cats like
to eat for breakfast?**
Mice Krispies

**How can you tell if you
have a stupid dog?**
It chases parked cars

**What do cat actors
say on stage?**
'Tabby or not tabby?'

**What kind of dog
does Dracula have?**
A bloodhound

**What happened to the dog
that ate nothing but garlic?**
*His bark was much
worse than his bite*

**What happens when it's
raining cats and dogs?**
You can step in a poodle

**What did the parrot say
to the spaniel?**
'I'm a cocker too.'

**What do you get if you cross a
dog with a maze?**
A labyrinth

**What do you get if you
cross a Jack Russell
with a vegetable?**
A Jack Brussells sprout

**What do you get if you cross a
dog with a chicken?**
Pooched eggs

When is it bad luck to see a black cat?
When you're a mouse

What do you call a guinea pig with three eyes?
Guinea piiig

**What does a kitten become
after it's three days old?**
Four days old

GIRL: I lost my dog.
BOY: *Why don't you put an
ad in the newspaper?*
GIRL: Don't be silly!
He can't read.

**What do you do if your pet
swallows your pencil?**
Use a pen

**What happened to the cat that
swallowed a ball of wool?**
She had mittens

What did the dog say to the hot dog bun?
'Are you pure bred?'

What do you call a rabbit that has fleas?
Bugs Bunny

What is a rabbit's favourite kind of music?
Hip-Hop

A policeman stopped a car. There was a donkey in the front seat with the driver. 'What are you doing with that donkey? You should take it to the zoo,' he said. The following week, the same policeman saw the same

man with the donkey in the front seat again, with both of them wearing sunglasses. The policeman pulled him over and said, 'I thought you were going to take that donkey to the zoo!' The man replied, 'I did. We had such a great time that we are going to the beach this weekend!'

What sound does a cat on the motorway make?
Miaooooooooooow

What did the hungry Dalmatian say when she finished her dinner?
'That hit the spots!'

What did the cat say when he spent all his money?
'I'm paw!'

How do you get a dog to stop digging in the garden?
Take away his shovel

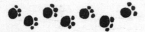

Who is a cat's favourite singer?
Kitty Perry

What dog loves to take bubble baths?
A shampoodle

Slippery and slimy

Where do frogs keep their money?
In a river bank

**What do you say to a
hitch-hiking frog?**
'Hop in!'

**What do you get when you
cross a snake and a pie?**
A pie-thon

**How can you tell if a
snake is a baby?**
It has a rattle

**What kind of shoes
do frogs wear?**
Open toad

**What do you get if you cross
a snake with a pig?**
A boar constrictor

What animal has more lives than the cat?
A frog, as he croaks every night

What do you call a sick crocodile?
An illigator

What do you get if you cross a crocodile with a camera?
A snap-shot

What's green and can jump a mile a minute?
A frog with hiccups

What is the best thing to do if you find a crocodile in your bed?
Sleep somewhere else

**What's sweet but
has sharp teeth?**
A chocodile

**What do you get if you cross a
crocodile with a flower?**
*I don't know, but I'm not
going to smell it*

**What kind of tiles can't
you stick on walls?**
Reptiles

**What do you call a girl
with a frog on her head?**
Lily

What's a snake's favourite subject at school?
Hissssstory

What kind of lizard tells jokes?
A stand-up chameleon

A kid walks into the classroom with a newt on his shoulder. The teacher asks, 'What's that on your shoulder?' The kid replies, 'That's my pet newt, Tiny.' The teacher says, 'Why do you call him Tiny?' The kid says, 'Because he is my newt!'

What do you call
a thieving alligator?
A crookodile

What is a frog's
favourite drink?
Croaka-Cola

**What did the traffic warden
say to the frog that was
parked illegally?**
'Hop it, or you'll be toad.'

**What do you call a snake
with no clothes on?**
Snaked

Why are frogs so happy?
*Because they eat everything
that bugs them*

**What do snakes have
on their bath towels?**
Hiss and Hers

**What do you get if you
cross a toad with a galaxy?**
Star warts

**Why can't you teach
a frog to sing?**
Because old ribbits die hard

**Why didn't the female
frog lay eggs?**
*Because her partner
spawned her affections*

**Rabbits can multiply, but
only a snake can be an adder.**

**Which animal
discovered gravity?**
Sir Isaac Newt-on

**How do you confuse
a chameleon?**
Put him on a tartan rug

What do frogs do with paper?
Rip-it

**What is a frog's
favourite game?**
Croaket

Bird Brains

Who wrote Great Eggspectations?
Charles Chickens

TEACHER: What's a robin?
PUPIL: *A bird that steals, Miss.*

What books do owls read?
Hoot-dunnits

What happened when the turkey got into a fight?
He got the stuffing knocked out of him

BOY: My canary died of flu.
GIRL: *I didn't know canaries got flu.*
BOY: Mine flew into a car.

Knock, knock
Who's there?
Toucan!
Toucan who?
Toucan play this game!

**What do you get if you cross
an eagle with a skunk?**
A bird that stinks to high heaven

**What do birds use
to help them land?**
Sparrowchutes

What do you give a sick bird?
Tweetment

**What do you call a parrot
that's flown away?**
A polly-gone

**How do crows stick
together in a flock?**
Velcrow

**What should you write on a
chicken's gravestone?**
'Roast in Peace'

**What do you get when you
cross a parrot with a pig?**
A bird who hogs the conversation

**Why did the chicken
cross the road?**
*To show everyone he
wasn't chicken*

Why didn't the skeleton chicken cross the road?
Because he didn't have the guts

Why don't Batman and Robin go fishing?
Because Robin eats all the worms

What do you get when you cross a shark and a parrot?
I don't know, but it would talk your ear off

What do you get from a drunken chicken?
Scotch eggs

**Where do birds invest
their money?**
In the stork market

**What did the duck say when
she bought a lipstick?**
Put it on my bill

**Why did the chicken
cross the playground?**
To get to the other slide

**What do you get when you
cross a parrot
with a centipede?**
A walkie talkie

Which seabird can dance?
A pelican-can

**Why didn't the chicken
cross the road?**
*Because there was a KFC
on the other side*

**Who tells the best
chicken jokes?**
The comedi-hen

TEACHER: Name a bird with
wings that can't fly.
PUPIL: *A dead bird, sir.*

Why do hummingbirds hum?
*Because they don't
know the words*

**What kind of maths
do birds like?**
Owlgebra

**What do you call a bird
that's always out of breath?**
A puffin

**What do owls say
when it's raining?**
Too-wet-to-woo

**What do you call a
duck that steals?**
A robber duck

**What do you call an owl
with a deep voice?**
A growl

Why can't an emu fly?
Because it never books a flight

What do ducks like to eat?
Quackers

**Did you hear the joke
about the broken egg?**
It will crack you up

**What do you call a bird
in the winter?**
A brrr-d

**Why don't you see
penguins in Britain?**
Because they're afraid of Wales

**How do you know owls are
smarter than chickens?**
*Have you ever heard of
Kentucky Fried Owls?*

When should you buy a bird?
When it's going cheep

Under the Sea

**Where do sharks go
on their holidays?**
Finland

**What happened to
the octopus who deserted
from the army?**
He had to face the firing squid

**Why do fish have such
big phone bills?**
*Because once they get on
the line they can't get off*

**What do you do with
a blue whale?**
Try to cheer him up

**Where does a lobster
keep his clothes?**
In the clawset

**What's the difference between
a fish and a piano?**
You can't tuna fish

What do whales eat?
Fish and ships

**If you had three octopuses
in your wallet, how
rich would you be?**
You'd be squids in

**Why did the crab
go to prison?**
*Because he was always
pinching things*

Why are fish so smart?
Because they live in schools

Two fish are in a tank. One turns to the other and says, 'Hey, do you know how to drive this thing?'

What did the lobster say to the mermaid?
Nothing, lobsters can't talk

Does a dolphin ever do something by accident?
No, they always do everything on porpoise

What does a clam do on its birthday?
Shellabrate

What did the fish say when he swam into a wall?
'Dam.'

Why did the plaice go to the doctor?
Because he was feeling a bit flat

What do you call a
fish with no eyes?
A fsh

What's an eel's
favourite dance move?
The conger line

What day of the week
do fish hate?
Fry-day

Which fish do you take to a fight?
A swordfish

What do you call a baby whale?
A little squirt

Who granted the fish's wish?
The fairy codmother

Why are fish so gullible?
*They fall for things hook,
line and sinker*

**Why is it easy to spot
Cinderella-fish?**
They have glass flippers

**What do you call fish that
sing songs at Christmas?**
Coral singers

**Where does a whale
play her flute?**
In the orca-stra

**What kind of fish will
help you hear better?**
A herring aid

**Why couldn't Noah
catch many fish when
he was on the Ark?**
He only had two worms

**What's a fish's favourite
party games?**
*Bass The Parcel, Name That
Tuna, and Tide and Seek*

What's the laziest fish?
A kipper

Where do baby fish go every morning?
To plaice-school